# The Castl

Written by Alasdair Hutton

Illustrated by William Gorman

Published by Foggie Toddle Books

*The little cat liked eating fish*
*friendly soldiers grant his wish*
*I hope you enjoy this little tale*

*Alasdair Hutton*

This book is dedicated to

**Fergus Hutton - AH**
**Erik - WG**

The moral rights of the author and illustrator have been asserted in
accordance with the Copyright, Designs and Patents Act 1988.
ISBN: 978-1-8380-3790-1
Published by Foggie Toddle Books
18 North Main Street, Wigtown DG8 9HL
01988 402896
hello@foggietoddlebooks.co.uk

The smell of fish and chips brought the little cat out of his hiding place. He lived in a small village in Scotland, but not in a comfortable house, his hiding place was under some rusting corrugated iron in the corner of an old, ruined cottage.

Every day the kitten had to go out and look for something to eat, being careful to look out for bigger cats and neighbourhood dogs. As the scent from the nearby fish and chip shop drifted on the evening air it made the kitten feel very hungry and he remembered that he could scrounge some scraps from the kitchen.

The little cat crept carefully out of his hiding place and followed the lovely smell. He kept a wary eye open and noticed that the only customers in the shop were two soldiers in camouflage clothes. They were buying enough fish suppers for six people.

Soldiers were usually generous, the kitten thought, and decided that he would follow them in the hope they would drop something or throw him a scrap of fish as they ate. But they packed their purchase in a special space blanket to keep it hot, stowed it in a backpack and set off at a jog trot.

The little cat decided he would follow them, but the soldiers did not stop until they reached their four friends who were rigging up small tents on a grassy spot by a burn. By then the little cat had gone a long way from home and he was too tired to turn back.

"Right lads, scoff," announced one of the two soldiers who had bought the fish and chips. The others all stopped as the food was unwrapped, and each fish supper was handed out.

"Hello, what have we got here?" the leader of the patrol asked, spotting the little cat. Where have you come from?" "Och, he followed us up from the village," said the soldier who had carried the suppers.

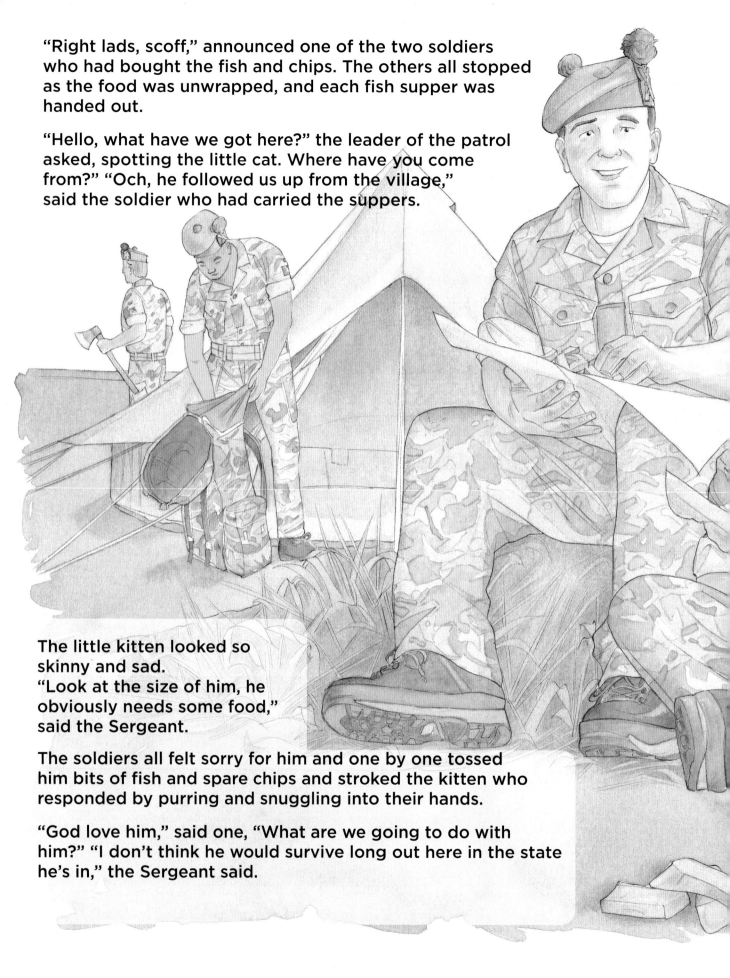

The little kitten looked so skinny and sad.
"Look at the size of him, he obviously needs some food," said the Sergeant.

The soldiers all felt sorry for him and one by one tossed him bits of fish and spare chips and stroked the kitten who responded by purring and snuggling into their hands.

"God love him," said one, "What are we going to do with him?" "I don't think he would survive long out here in the state he's in," the Sergeant said.

They all agreed they should adopt the kitten as a mascot and take him back to their barracks which were in the famous castle of Scotland's capital city.

At Edinburgh Castle the soldiers found him a warm, snug place to live close to their billets. In return the kitten kept the rooms where the soldiers lived clear of the mice who were often quite a nuisance when they chewed the soldiers' belongings.

As he grew stronger the kitten became bolder and started to explore. His soldier friends would go out each day quite early and he began to leave the place where he slept and stalk along corridors and up and down stairs. Edinburgh Castle was huge. There were tall buildings towering above him everywhere and he did not know what lay round each corner, but he was keen to find out.

Because he had first seen the world in a highland village, the kitten had to get used to the crowds of people who visited the Castle every day.

They did not always look where they were going but he was curious by nature and after a few days the little cat learned how to move carefully among them to avoid being trodden on!

As he grew more confident, he went up the hill in short dashes when there were gaps between the feet, coming out right at the top of the Castle and he peeped through one of the gun ports in the Half Moon Battery, which he thought was a window.

Far below he could see nothing but buildings of all shapes and sizes stretching far into the distance. This was amazing, he'd never seen anything like it, it really was another world.

Boom! The little cat almost jumped out of his skin! What was that?

Were they under attack? Was this why the soldiers lived here wondered the little cat as he shivered and shook from the bang.

He soon learned that it was the One O'Clock Gun, fired each day to mark that hour. Many people in the Castle and the city below set their watches by the regular firing.

On his new diet of food from the soldiers and scraps dropped by the Castle visitors, the kitten soon grew strong and healthy. He liked to go on patrol and one warm day he was taking a break, basking in the sun and watching a family gathered to see the gun being fired.

But the little girl in the group hadn't realised how loud it would be and as the shot rang out she jumped just as the little cat had the first time. The pound coin she'd been holding tightly to spend in the Castle Shop went flying into the air spinning round in the sunshine before rolling away. The little girl's crying could be heard all over the Castle!

But the little cat had seen it all and as it flew into the air; he'd leapt from his warm seat and chased after the coin as it rolled this way and that. He weaved in and out of passing feet, just missing the coin as it kept rolling down the hill. His quick little paws eventually stopped the coin and flattened it to the ground.

He carefully picked it up with his teeth and trotted proudly back up the hill to where the little girl was being comforted by her grandparents who had given her the money to spend.

"Look" said the little girl's Grandma, "This little cat has just dropped something at your feet...goodness me it's your coin!" Everyone was so surprised. The little girl went over to the cat and stretched out her hand to stroke him. "Thank you, little cat," she said softly. "You're so clever, you are my champion. I shall call you the Castle Cat."

The little cat jumped up onto the One O'Clock Gun where everyone gathered to stroke him, he purred loudly at all the attention. Picking up his granddaughter who held her coin tightly in her hand, the Grandfather shouted: "Three cheers for the Castle Cat" and everyone started to applaud the cat as well.

If you could see a cat blush you would have noticed the kitten turn pink with pride; he really did belong here, he was now the Castle Cat!

## ALASDAIR HUTTON

Alasdair Hutton has been writing since he was in primary school. This is his fifth book for children and follows the early life of the Castle Cat which he first created in the Tattoo Fox book in 2013.

Alasdair, who lives in the Scottish Borders, emigrated to Australia at the age of 14 and started his working life in a local radio station. He later became a newspaper reporter in Australia and continued as a reporter when he returned to Scotland. Then he moved to the BBC as an announcer until he was elected as the first Member of the European Parliament for the South of Scotland. Later he was elected as a local Councillor in the Scottish Borders.

He was a volunteer paratrooper for 22 years and now helps to raise money for service veterans' welfare. He was appointed as writer and storyteller of the Royal Edinburgh Military Tattoo in 1992 and had not missed a performance until the pandemic interrupted the event.

He would like to dedicate this little book to Fergus Hutton.

## WILLIAM GORMAN

Artist William Gorman studied Illustration and Printmaking at the Duncan of Jordanstone College of Art and Design in Dundee.

After graduating he spent time travelling before returning to Galloway to begin a career as an artist and illustrator. He lives and works in Wigtown, Scotland's National Booktown. Known for his skill depicting dogs this is William's first venture into illustrating cats.

This is his second children's book working with writer Alasdair Hutton.

# EDINBURGH CASTLE

Edinburgh Castle is one of the most famous buildings in the world. It is the oldest continuously inhabited place in the British Isles. The rock it stands on was formed by a volcano some 340 million years ago and there have been people living on it for at least 3000 years.

The awesome stronghold has seen some of the great events of Scottish history and for centuries it was a formidable stronghold of royal power. During the bloody Wars of Independence with England in the early fourteenth century, it passed back and forth between the Scots and the English before it finally settled in Scottish hands. Its most historic happening occurred in June 1566 when Mary Queen of Scots gave birth to Prince James, who grew up to become the king who united the Crowns of Scotland and England in 1603. Bonnie Prince Charlie tried and failed to capture the Castle in the Jacobite rebellion of 1745 and peace has reigned over the great fortress ever since.

Today the castle is Scotland's biggest visitor attraction. Inside are the country's crown jewels, the Crown, the Sword and the Sceptre, once hidden away to escape destruction by Oliver Cromwell but re-discovered by Sir Walter Scott and now proudly on display to the world.

Every day at one o'clock a gun is fired from the Castle battlements as a historic reminder of the days when it was needed to help sailors set their clocks before they set sail.

Each summer visitors from all over the globe come to see the famous Royal Edinburgh Military Tattoo performed on the esplanade in front of the Castle which is still home to soldiers from the Royal Regiment of Scotland, a super-regiment formed from six historic old Scottish Regiments in the early 21st century.

Foggie Toddle Books is an independent bookshop and publishing company based in Wigtown, Scotland's National Booktown.

Together with the imprint Second Sands Publishing, we publish poetry and non-fiction for adults and picture books for children.

**More information at www.foggietoddlebooks.co.uk**

## Other books by Alasdair Hutton

The Tattoo Fox
The Tattoo Fox Makes New Friends
The Greatest Show on Earth
Luath Treasury of Scottish Nursery Rhymes
Mustard and Pepper

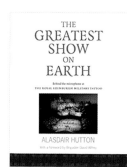
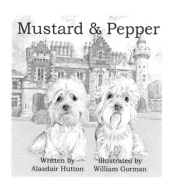